MW00962391

SHELBY TOWNSHIP LIBRARY
3 1515 00095 6?44

Pollinating a Flower

Paul Bennett

Thomson Learning
New York

Nature's Secrets

Catching a Meal
Changing Shape
Hibernation
Making a Nest
Migration
Pollinating a Flower

Cover: A colorful hummingbird pollinates the flower from which it feeds.

Title page: A soldier beetle crouches on a primrose willow.

Contents page: A sugar glider feeds on flowers.

First published in the
United States in 1994 by
Thomson Learning
115 Fifth Avenue
New York, NY 10003

Published simultaneously in
Great Britain by
Wayland (Publishers) Ltd.

Library of Congress Cataloging-in-Publication Data
Bennett, Paul, 1954–
Pollinating a flower / Paul Bennett.
p. cm.—(Nature's secrets)
Includes bibliographical references (p.) and index.
ISBN 1-56847-206-4
1. Pollination—Juvenile literature. [1. Pollination]
I. Title. II. Series: Bennett, Paul, 1954– Nature's secrets.
QK926.B42 1994
582'.01662—dc20 94-12198

Printed in Italy

Picture acknowledgments
The publishers would like to thank the following for allowing their photographs to be reproduced in this book: Bruce Coleman/John Shaw 4, H. J. Flugel 13 (bottom), Adrian Davies 25, Eric Crichton 29 (top); FLPA/Silvestris 10 (left), W. Broadhurst 10 (right), Jean Hosking 11 (top), W. Roberts 15; NHPA/John Shaw *title page*, Henry Ausloos 5 (top), Stephen Dalton 5 (center), 21, 24, 27, John Buckingham 5 (inset), Laurie Campbell 9, 11 (bottom), Eric Soder 9, G. J. Cambridge 14, Anthony Barrister 16, Jany Sauvanet 23, Elizabeth MacAndrew 26 (bottom); Oxford Scientific Films Ltd./Stephen Dalton *cover*, Belinda Wright *contents page*, Deni Brown 6, Harold Taylor 8, Kjell Sandved 17, David Thompson 19 (top), John Cooke 19 (bottom), 22 (bottom), Robert A. Tyrell 20, Gerald Thompson 22 (top), Jerome Wexler 26 (top), G. A. MacLean 29 (bottom); Science Photo Library/Claude Nuridsany and Marie Perennou 12, 13 (top), 18, Philippe Plailly 28.

Contents

The importance of flowers

Flowers are one of the most important parts of a plant. They make the seeds that grow into new plants. There are many different kinds of flowers. Some plants have just one flower each, while others produce a number of small flowers clustered together.

△ A dandelion flower is visited by a honeybee. After it is pollinated, the flower forms a fluffy seed head, which you can see on page 9.

These are the flowers and fruits of the broom plant. ▷

△ The wild rose forms fruits called "hips." The hips contain seeds from which new wild rose plants will grow. ▷

What is pollination?

Before a flower can make seeds, it must first be pollinated and fertilized. This can only happen when pollen grains from the male part of a flower land on a female flower. This is called pollination.

A flower is made up of many parts. The male parts of a flower are called stamens. At the tip of each stamen is an anther, which makes the pollen. The female part of a flower is called the pistil. A pistil is made up of a stigma, a tubelike style, and an ovary that contains egg cells.

△ This lily has a purple pistil and orange stamens.

After a flower has been pollinated, it can make seeds. The pollen grains go down the style from the stigma to the ovary. There, the male cells in the pollen grains fertilize the female cells to form seeds. A fruit with seeds then develops.

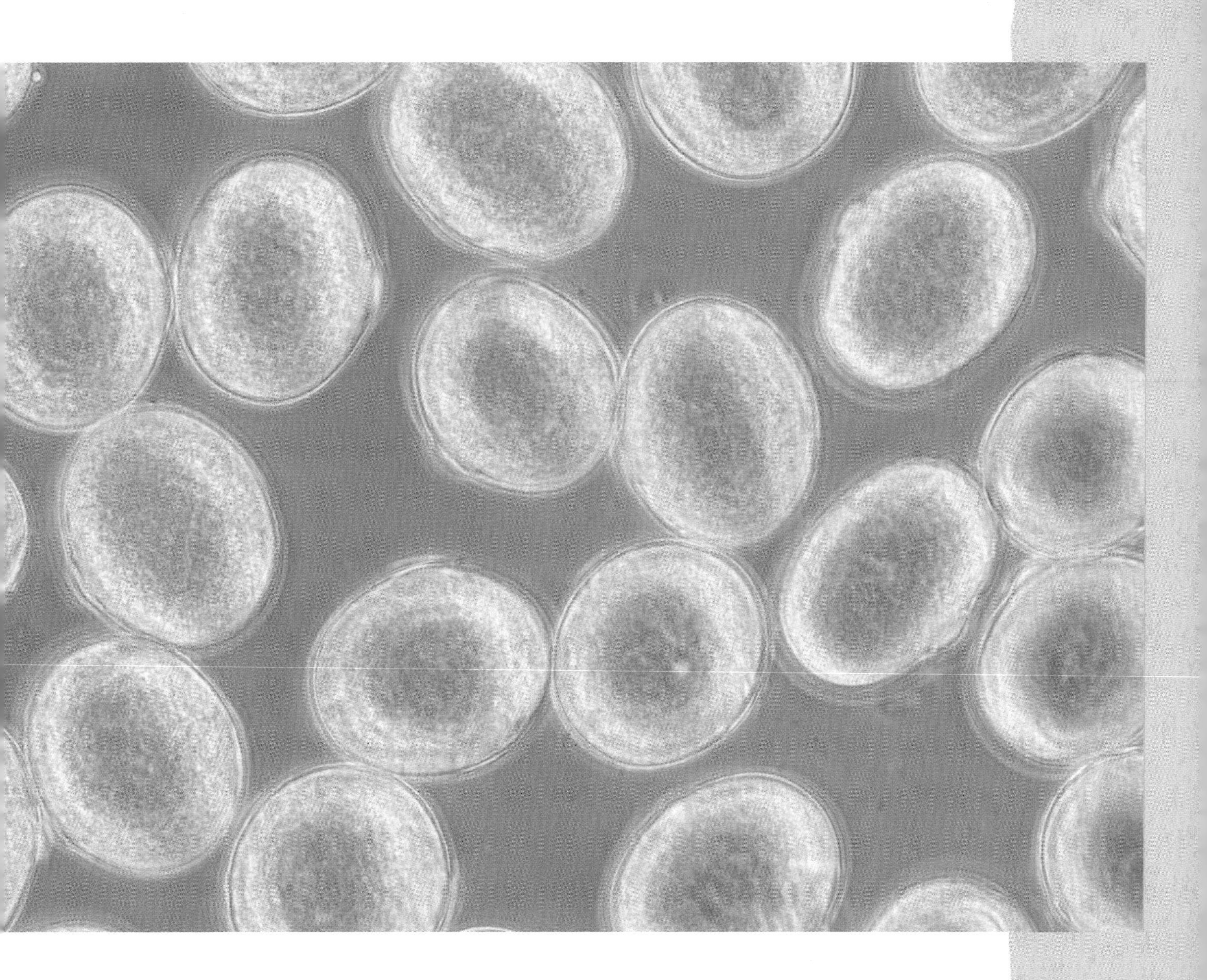

△ Pollen grains are so small that they look like tiny specks. This picture of sweet pea pollen has been taken through a microscope.

◁ Find the pistil and the stamens in this tulip.

△ After pollination, the seeds of a dandelion flower begin to grow. They each have a feathery parachute to help them float through the air.

Self-pollination

Most plants are pollinated by pollen from another plant of the same kind. This is called cross-pollination. But some plants have flowers that can pollinate themselves. This is called self-pollination.

◁ The male and female parts of many flowers are close together. If they ripen at the same time, the plant can pollinate itself. Some types of string beans are self-pollinating.

Oats are self-pollinating. ▷

△ Cotton is grown in the southern United States. It is a self-pollinating plant.

Some violets can pollinate themselves. ▷

Pollination by insects

Many flowers have male and female parts that ripen at different times. That way, the flowers avoid pollinating themselves. Instead, they must be cross-pollinated. One way to do this is to attract insects. As the insects crawl around on the flower their bodies pick up pollen from the stamens. Then, when they visit a similar type of flower, some of this pollen may land on the stigma and the flower will become pollinated.

△ Some insects are attracted by brightly colored flowers. They especially like yellow, purple, and pink. A brilliant cuckoo wasp feeds eagerly on nectar, the sweet-tasting liquid that is found at the base of the petals of many flowers.

△ This shiny beetle is feeding on the anthers of a wild rose flower. Like nectar, pollen is the food of many insects.

In their endless buzzing from plant to plant, honeybees pollinate many different types of flowers. They make honey from nectar and use pollen for food, which they collect in pollen baskets on their hind legs. ▷

Some flowers, such as this hemp nettle, have spotted markings or stripes of color that lead the insect to the nectar at the center of the flower. These markings are called nectar guides. ▽

Sweet-smelling flowers attract insects, too. Butterflies have a very good sense of smell. They also have long tongues that can suck up nectar from deep, tubelike flowers. ▷

◁ Flowers that are pollinated by night-flying moths, such as this hawk moth, send out their beautiful scent at night. The flowers are often pale so that they show up well in the dark.

△ But not all flowers smell sweet. This is the world's largest flower, rafflesia. It stinks of rotten meat to attract flies that will carry off the pollen grains.

Some flowers have specially shaped petals so that insects can easily land on them to feed.

△ The Spanish broom flower is well shaped for pollination by bees. The lower petal acts as a landing place and, as the bee climbs in looking for nectar, the anthers curl back, dusting the bee with pollen. At the same time, the sticky stigma picks up pollen left on the bee by another flower.

△ Some plants trick insects to pollinate them. The bee orchid looks and smells so much like a female bee that a male bee will land and try to mate with it. As the bee flies off, it carries some pollen with it to the next flower. ▷

Unlikely pollinators

In some parts of the world, birds and small animals pollinate flowers. Like insects, they visit the flowers to feed on sweet-smelling nectar or pollen. Flowers pollinated by birds are often bright red – a color that most insects cannot see.

◁ A colorful hummingbird hovers skillfully in front of a hibiscus flower. As it feeds on the sweet nectar, its head touches the anthers and is brushed with pollen. At the same time, the stigma collects pollen left on the bird by another flower. The long beak of the hummingbird makes it ideal for reaching deep inside tube-shaped flowers for nectar. As these birds feed, they transfer pollen from one flower to another.

△ In tropical countries, some bats, such as this short-tailed leaf-nosed bat, visit flowers to feed on pollen and nectar. Unlike most other flowers, bat-pollinated flowers open up at night.

△ In Australia, the tiny honey possum lives entirely on the nectar and pollen of flowers. It has a long snout and a brush-like tongue for collecting food.

◁ A South African rock mouse feeds on a flower. Some small rodents are pollinators.

Occasionally, large animals pollinate flowers in their search for food. This red howler monkey has pollen on its forehead after feeding on flowers. ▷

Blown by the wind

In spring and summer, the air around us is filled with tiny pollen grains floating in the wind. Since they do not need to attract insects to them, wind-pollinated flowers are mostly small and pale.

◁ Grass plants shed many millions of small, light pollen grains, but only a few of these find female flowers and fertilize them.

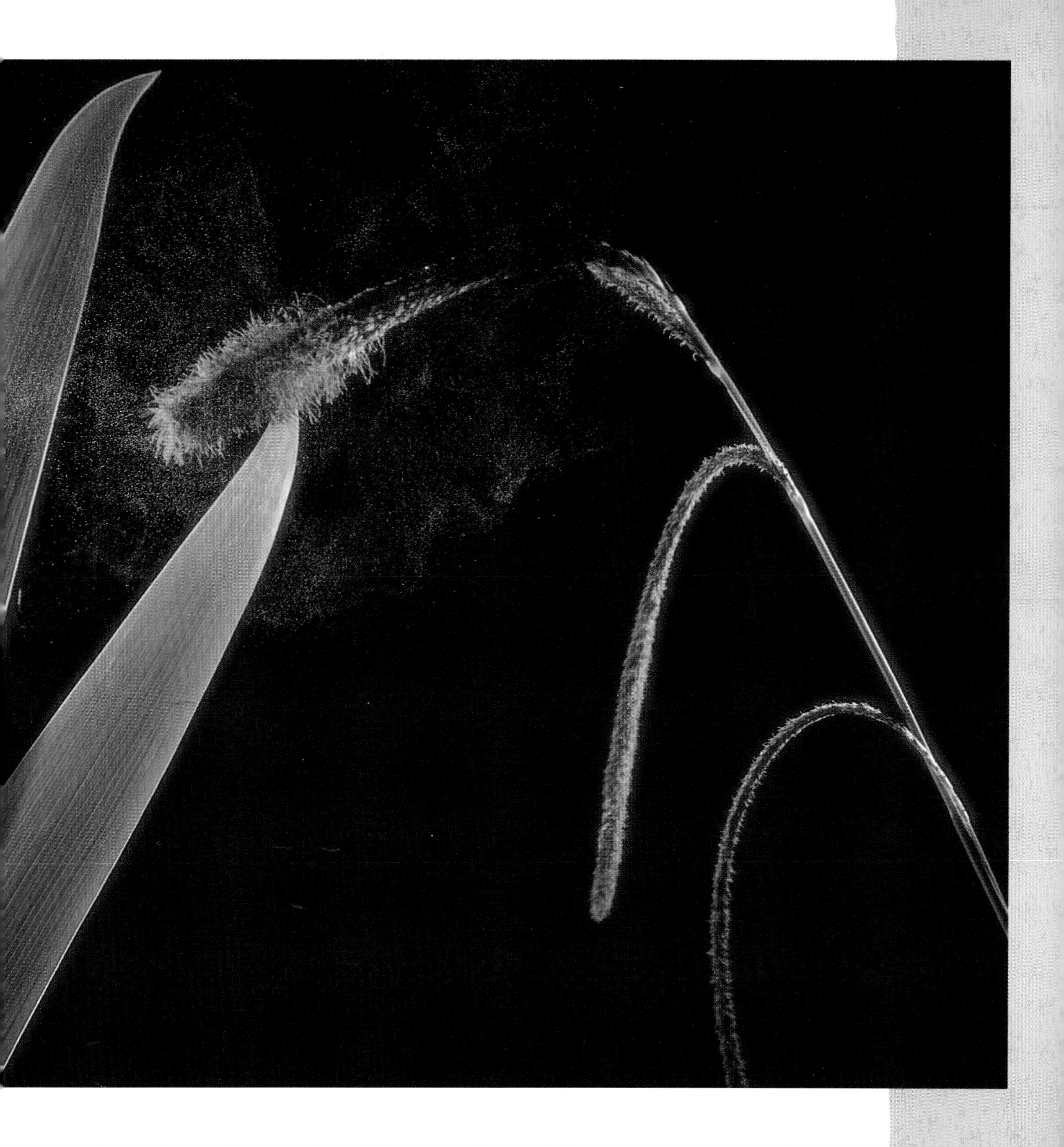

△ A sedge plant shedding pollen. The stamens and anthers of many grassy plants are feathery. The pollen floats in the air and is caught by the sticky stigma part of a female plant.

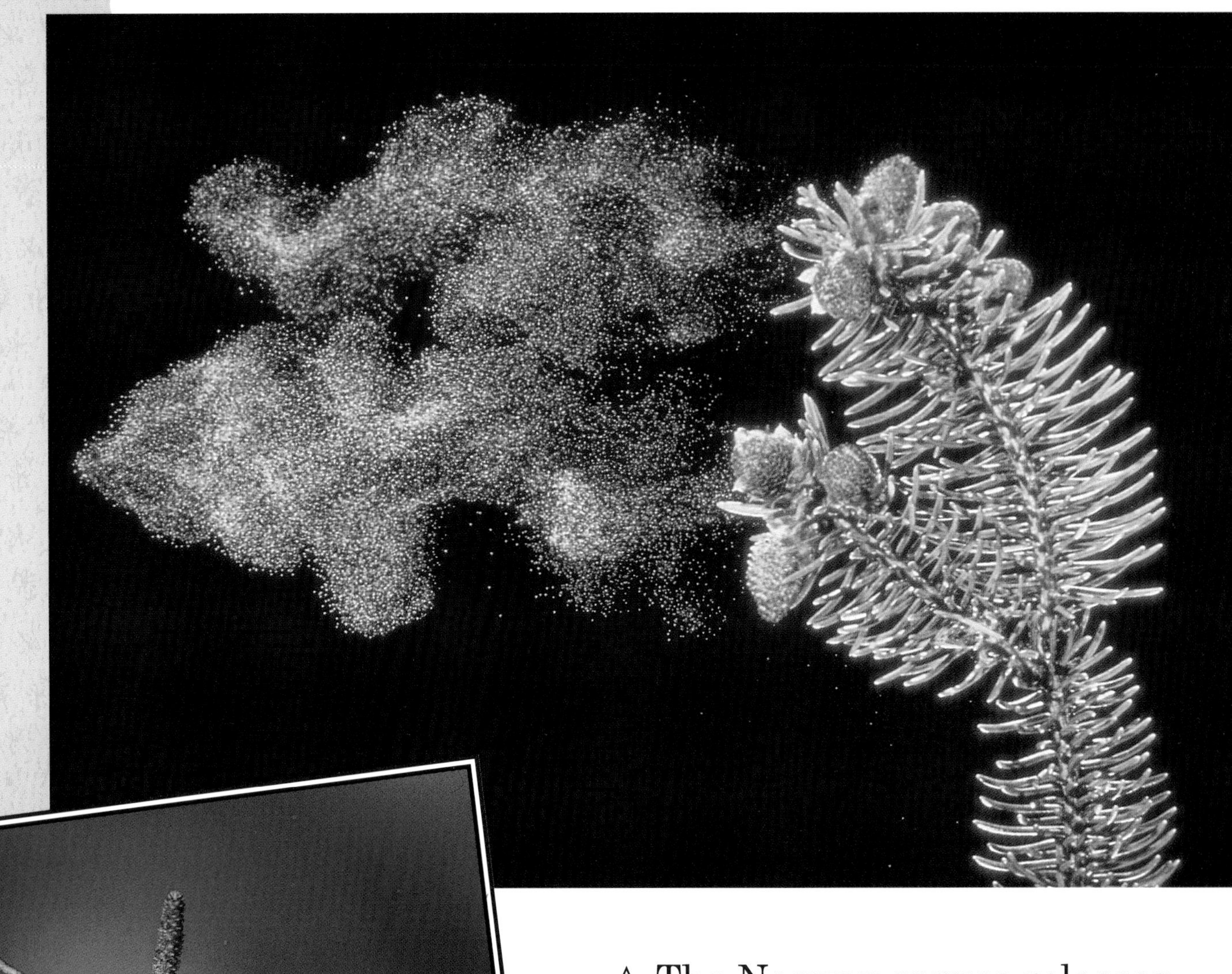

△ The Norway spruce releases a cloud of pollen. Many trees are wind pollinated.

◁ The silver birch has flower clusters called catkins. The catkins contain separate male and female flowers.

Hazel catkins release their pollen as they dangle in the wind. ▷

Pollination by people

Botanists – people who study plants – can create new varieties of plants by using artificial pollination. They do this to make the new plants resistant to disease or produce larger fruits.

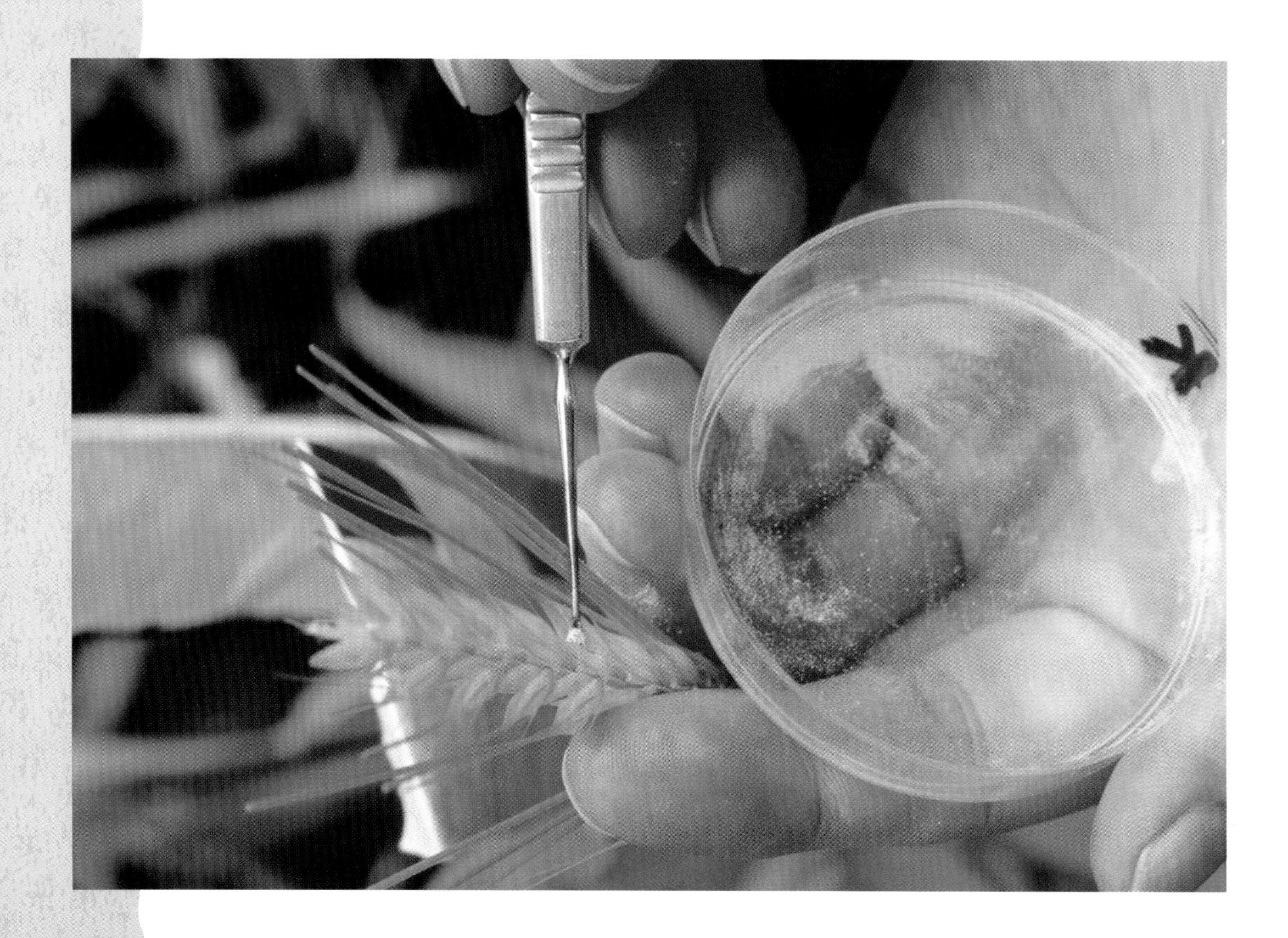

△ Wheat is a type of grass. Botanists have produced plants that can grow with very little water and have large grains for grinding into flour.

Botanists like to breed flowers that are very different in color or shape from ones found in the wild. Here some pollen is being transferred delicately from the anther of one flower to the stigma of another flower. ▷

A farmer has placed some beehives in an orchard. That way the flowers are sure to be pollinated and there will be a good crop of fruit. ▽

Glossary

Anther The upper part of the stamen. It produces pollen.

Artificial Made by people.

Breed To produce a plant or animal under controlled conditions.

Cells The smallest living units and the "building blocks" with which all plants and animals are made.

Fertilize When the male and female sex cells of a flower join together so that a seed may grow.

Fruits The parts of plants containing seeds.

Orchard A large area of fruit trees.

Ovary The female part of the flower containing the egg cells.

Pistil The female part of the flower consisting of the stigma, style, and ovary.

Pollen The yellow powdery grains made by male flowers. Pollen is needed by female flowers to make seeds.

Pollination The transfer of pollen from the anther to the stigma of a flower.

Ripen To become fully developed.

Rodents Animals, such as squirrels, beavers, and mice, that gnaw with their front teeth.

Seed The part of a plant from which a new plant may be grown.

Snout The nose and mouth of an animal.

Stamen The male part of the flower.

Stigma The female part of a flower that receives pollen.

Books to read

Kahkonen, Sharon. *Honey Bees.* Real Readers. Milwaukee: Raintree Steck-Vaughn, 1989.

Landau, Elaine. *Wildflowers Around the World.* First Books. New York: Franklin Watts, 1991.

Mayes, S. *What Makes a Flower Grow?* Tulsa, OK: EDC Publishing, 1989.

Meadway, Wendy. *Let's Look at Birds.* Let's Look At. New York: Bookwright Press, 1990.

Morgan, Nina. *The Plant Cycle.* Natural Cycles. New York: Thomson Learning, 1993.

Mound, Lawrence. *Insect.* New York: Alfred A. Knopf Books for Young Readers, 1990.

Sabin, Louis. *Plants, Seeds & Flowers.* Mahwah, NJ: Troll Associates, 1985.

Stidworthy, John. *Flowers, Trees and Other Plants.* New York: Random House Books for Young Readers, 1991.

Projects

Project: **Insect Pollinators**

You can observe insects as they pollinate flowers in your backyard. If you do not have a backyard, you can visit a park. Make a note of how many different types of insects visit the flowers. Watch one butterfly and record how many flowers it visits. If you have more than one type of butterfly visit your yard, do they visit the same type of flower or do they prefer different flowers? Observe a bee in the same way.

Keep a diary of your observations. Draw or photograph the flowers in your yard. Which flowers are the most popular? Do the insects prefer flowers of a particular color? Keep a record of the time of day that different insects visit. You can also record the weather and the time of year. In some parts of the world, some butterflies are becoming rare because of the loss of their habitat. You can attract butterflies to your backyard by having the right flowering plants, such as buddleia or butterfly weed.

Project: **Pollen Grains**

Pollen grains are very tiny and look like dust. However, they can vary greatly in shape and size. You can look at pollen grains under a microscope (see page 7). Collect a small amount of pollen from one of the flowers in your garden. Hold the microscope slide near the stamen and tap the head gently. Some pollen grains should fall onto the slide. Now look at the pollen grains under the microscope.

Collect pollen from other flowers and observe them in the same way. Compare the size, shape, and color of the different pollen grains. Add these observations to your diary. You can also draw the shape of the different pollen grains.

Index

SHELBY